Bless You!

by Sheryl Webster

Illustrated by Tomislav Zlatic

W
FRANKLIN WATTS
LONDON•SYDNEY

First published in 2010 by
Franklin Watts
338 Euston Road
London
NW1 3BH

Franklin Watts Australia
Level 17/207 Kent Street
Sydney
NSW 2000

A CIP catalogue record for this book is available
from the British Library.

ISBN 978 0 7496 9429 6 (hbk)
ISBN 978 0 7496 9434 0 (pbk)

Series Editor: Jackie Hamley
Series Advisor: Catherine Glavina
Series Designer: Peter Scoulding

Printed in China

Franklin Watts is a division of
Hachette Children's Books,
an Hachette UK company
www.hachette.co.uk

For my husband Phil and our children
Sean, Bethany, Joey and Katy – S.W. x

All was quiet in the jungle.

And then ...

... Elephant set off
for her walk.

THUMP

THUMP

4

She thumped along and soon she
saw Tiger trying to fly his kite.
But there was no breeze at all.
The kite flopped to the ground.

"What a lovely kite," said Elephant.

"Can I help you to fly it?" she asked.

"No, thank you," said Tiger.

"Sorry!" said Elephant.

Elephant plodded on feeling
a little sad. She wished that
she could help Tiger.

Then she came to the lake and saw Zebra trying to sail her boat. But there was not even a little puff of wind. So the boat just floated there and did not move.

"What a great boat," said Elephant.

"Can I help you to sail it?" she asked.

"No, thank you," said Zebra.

"Sorry!" said Elephant.

Elephant plodded on feeling very sad. She wished that she could help Zebra.

Elephant came to a tree and saw Parrot trying to show her children how to fly. But it would take a gale to make them take off. The children were too scared to move.

"What brave children," said Elephant. "Can I help you to teach them?" she asked.

THUMP

"No, thank you," said Parrot.

"Sorry!" said Elephant. She plodded
on feeling very, very sad. She wished
that she could help Parrot.

Soon she heard a loud roar.

It was Lion and he was not happy.

He was trying to dry his messy wet mane. But it would take a gust to blow those locks dry.

Elephant tiptoed past as fast as she could. She felt so sad. "I wish that I could help Lion," she said to herself, "but I don't think that he would let me go near his lovely hair. I am too big and clumsy to help my friends."

19

She came to the water hole.
"A bath will make me feel
better," said Elephant.
So she rubbed the soap
and made some bubbles.
Then ... OH DEAR!

Her trunk got a tickle -
And ...

ATCHOOO

Elephant's sneeze
gusted past Lion ...

... howled past Parrot
and her children ...

… puffed past Zebra …

... and breezed past Tiger!

All of the animals were delighted.
"BLESS YOU!" they shouted.

Elephant felt very happy.

"I did help my friends after all!"

Put these pictures in the correct order.
Now try writing the story in your own words!

Puzzle 2

1. This mane will never dry.

2. I hate having my hair washed.

3. Let me help you, please!

4. I'm just too big and clumsy to join in.

5. Don't be afraid!

6. Come on, children, flap and jump!

Choose the correct speech bubbles for each character. Can you think of any others? Turn over to find the answers.

Answers

Puzzle 1

The correct order is: 1a, 2c, 3f, 4b, 5e, 6d

Puzzle 2

Elephant: 3, 4

Parrot: 5, 6

Lion: 1, 2

Look out for more great Hopscotch stories:

My Dad's a Balloon
ISBN 978 0 7496 9428 9*
ISBN 978 0 7496 9433 3

AbracaDebra
ISBN 978 0 7496 9427 2*
ISBN 978 0 7496 9432 6

Marigold's Bad Hair Day
ISBN 978 0 7496 9430 2*
ISBN 978 0 7496 9435 7

Mrs Bootle's Boots
ISBN 978 0 7496 9431 9*
ISBN 978 0 7496 9436 4

How to Teach a Dragon Manners
ISBN 978 0 7496 5873 1

The Best Den Ever
ISBN 978 0 7496 5876 2

The Princess and the Frog
ISBN 978 0 7496 5129 9

I Can't Stand It!
ISBN 978 0 7496 5765 9

The Truth about those Billy Goats
ISBN 978 0 7496 5766 6

Izzie's Idea
ISBN 978 0 7496 5334 7

Clever Cat
ISBN 978 0 7496 5131 2

"Sausages!"
ISBN 978 0 7496 4707 0

The Truth about Hansel and Gretel
ISBN 978 0 7496 4708 7

The Queen's Dragon
ISBN 978 0 7496 4618 9

Plip and Plop
ISBN 978 0 7496 4620 2

Find out more about all the Hopscotch books at:
www.franklinwatts.co.uk

*hardback